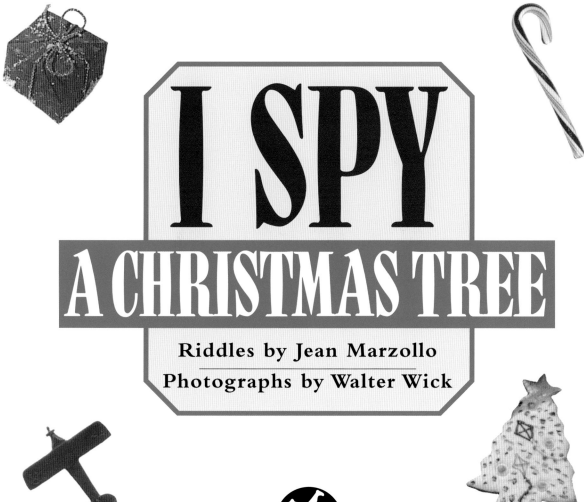

# I SPY
## A CHRISTMAS TREE

**Riddles by Jean Marzollo**

**Photographs by Walter Wick**

**Cartwheel** B·O·O·K·S ®

SCHOLASTIC INC.

New York   Toronto   London   Auckland
Sydney   Mexico City   New Delhi   Hong Kong

I spy

a top

and a Christmas tree;

I spy

two birds

and a present for me!

I spy

a parrot

and a horse that's red;

I spy

a sun face

and Santa's sled.

I spy

five candy canes

and a blue plane;

I spy

an ornament

and lights in a train.

I spy

a guitar

and a cookie clock;

I spy

an apple

and a 2 on a block.

I spy

a race car

and a Christmas cat;

I spy

a reindeer

and a Santa hat.

# I SPY Christmas Tree Hunt

Use your eyes, and take a look.
Find these trees throughout the book!

Big cookie tree

Little cookie tree

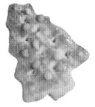

Little cookie tree

Candy wrapper tree

Wooden tree

# I SPY Rhyming Word Hunt

These words rhyme—can you hear?
Find them all and give a cheer!

Polar bear

Yellow van

Little duck

Golden hair

Policeman

Yellow truck

For Connor, Nolan, Emma, Hudson, Julia, Addyson, and James,
with grateful thanks to Dan and Dave — J.M.

For Victoria Hamel — W.W.

Directions for the *I Spy a Christmas Tree* ornaments:

- Punch out each ornament.
- Slide two matching circles together to create ornament.
- Use clear tape to secure the seams.
- Tie a string through the hole and hang on your tree.
- Play I Spy a Christmas Tree.

Text copyright © 2010 by Jean Marzollo
Cover illustration from *I Spy Christmas* © 1992 by Walter Wick; "Santa's Workshop" from *I Spy Christmas* © 1992 by Walter Wick;
"The Holly and the Ivy" from *I Spy Christmas* © 1992 by Walter Wick; "Stocking Stuffers" from *I Spy Christmas* © 1992 by Walter Wick;
"Ornaments" from *I Spy Christmas* © 1992 by Walter Wick; "Nutcracker Sweets" from *I Spy Christmas* © 1992 by Walter Wick;
"Silent Night" from *I Spy Christmas* © 1992 by Walter Wick; "Under the Tree" from *I Spy Christmas* © 1992 by Walter Wick;
"Winter Sports" from *I Spy Christmas* © 1992 by Walter Wick; "Window Shopping" from *I Spy Christmas* © 1992 by Walter Wick;

Library of Congress Cataloging-in-Publication Data

Marzollo, Jean.
  I spy a Christmas tree / by Jean Marzollo ; photographs by Walter Wick.
    p. cm.
  ISBN 978-0-545-22092-7
  1. Picture puzzles—Juvenile literature. 2. Christmas—Juvenile literature. I. Wick, Walter. II. Title.
  GV1507.P47M283 2010
  793.73—dc22
                                               2009032757

ISBN 978-0-545-22092-7

10 9 8 7 6 5 4 3 2 1                 10 11 12 13 14
Printed in Malaysia 108
First printing, September 2010